Frances Hodgson Burnett,
the author of this book,
later expanded the story
of Sara Crewe and
called it
A Little Princess

About the Author

Frances Hodgson Burnett was born in England in 1849. She began to tell stories soon after she learned to talk, and she wrote them down on scraps of paper as soon as she learned to write.

When Frances was four years old, her father died and a few years later the family ran out of money. An uncle in Tennessee invited them to come live with him. But by the time they arrived, he too had lost his money. All he had left was a little log cabin for them to live in.

It was then that Frances decided to sell her stories. To get the money to buy paper and stamps, she and her sisters picked wild grapes and sold them.

Her first story was published when she was thirteen. During the next sixty years she wrote fifty books. Some of them were written for children: *Sara Crewe, A Little Princess, Little Lord Fauntleroy,* and *The Secret Garden.*

Frances' life was a comfortable one when she grew up. She married a doctor and they had two sons. She was a generous woman and heaped expensive presents on everyone around her. Her gift to you? This book!

SARA CREWE

Frances Hodgson Burnett

Illustrations by Brian Wildsmith

AN
APPLE®
PAPERBACK

SCHOLASTIC INC.
New York Toronto London Auckland Sydney

ISBN 0-590-42323-1

12 11 10 9 8 7 6   2 3 4 5/9

Printed in the U.S.A.   40

Contents

Alone
in the World

In the first place, Miss Minchin lived in London. Her home was a large, dull, tall one, in a large, dull square, where all the houses were alike and all the sparrows were alike, and where all the door knockers made the same heavy sound and on still days — and nearly all the days were still — seemed to resound through the entire row in which the knock was knocked. On Miss

Minchin's door there was a brass plate. On the brass plate there was inscribed in black letters,

> **Miss Minchin's**
> **Select Seminary For Young Ladies**

Little Sara Crewe never went in or out of the house without reading that doorplate and reflecting upon it. By the time she was twelve, she had decided that all her trouble arose because, in the first place, she was not "Select," and in the second, she was not a "Young Lady." When she was eight years old, she had been brought to Miss Minchin as a pupil, and left with her.

Sara's papa brought her all the way from India. Her mamma had died when she was a baby, and her papa had kept her with him as long as he could. And then, finding the hot climate was making her very delicate, he had brought her to England and left her with Miss Minchin, to be part of the Select Seminary for Young Ladies. Sara, who had always been a sharp little child who remembered things, recollected hearing him say that he had not a relative in the world whom he knew of, and so he was obliged to place her at a boarding school, and he had heard Miss Minchin's establishment spoken of very highly. The same day, he took Sara out and bought her a great many beautiful clothes — clothes so grand and rich that only a very young and inexperienced man would have bought them for a mite of a child who was to be brought up in a boarding school. But the fact was that he was a rash, innocent young man, and very sad at the thought of parting with his little girl, who was all he had left to remind him of her beautiful mother, whom he had dearly loved. And he wished her to have everything the most fortunate little girl could have; and so when the polite sales-women in the shops said, "Here is our very latest thing in hats; the plumes are exactly the same as those we sold to Lady Diana Sinclair yesterday," he immediately bought what was offered to him and paid whatever was asked. The consequence was that Sara had a most extraordinary wardrobe. Her dresses were silk and velvet and India cashmere, her hats and bonnets were covered with bows and plumes, her small undergar-ments were adorned with real lace, and she returned in the cab to Miss Minchin's with a doll almost as large as herself and dressed quite as grandly as herself, too.

Then her papa gave Miss Minchin some money and went away, and for several days Sara would neither touch the doll, nor her breakfast, nor her dinner, nor her tea, and would do nothing but crouch in a small corner by the window and cry. She cried so much, in-deed, that she made herself ill. She was a queer little child, with old-fashioned ways and strong feelings, and she had adored her papa, and could not be made to think that India and an interesting bungalow were not better for her than London and Miss Minchin's Select Seminary. The instant she had entered the house, she had begun promptly to hate Miss Minchin and to think little of Miss Amelia Minchin, who was smooth and dumpy, and lisped, and was evidently afraid of her older sister. Miss Minchin was tall and had large, cold, fishy eyes, and large, cold hands which seemed fishy too because they were damp and made chills run down Sara's back when they touched her, as Miss Minchin pushed her hair off her forehead and said:

"A most beautiful and promising little girl, Captain Crewe. She will be a favorite pupil — *quite* a favorite pupil, I see."

For the first year she was a favorite pupil; at least she was indulged a great deal more than was good for her. And when the Select Seminary went walking, two by two, she was always decked out in her grandest clothes, and led by the hand, at the head of the genteel procession, by Miss Minchin herself. And when the parents of any of the pupils came, she was always dressed and called into the parlor with her doll; and she used to hear Miss Minchin say that her father was a distinguished Indian officer, and she would be heiress to a great fortune. That her father had inherited a great deal of money, Sara had heard before; and also that some day

it would be hers, and that he would not remain long in the army, but would come to live in London. And every time a letter came, she hoped it would say he was coming and they were to live together again.

But about the middle of the third year a letter came bringing very different news. Because he was not a businessman himself, her papa had given his affairs into the hands of a friend he trusted. The friend had deceived and robbed him. All the money was gone, no one knew exactly where, and the shock was so great to the poor, rash young officer that, being attacked by jungle fever shortly afterward, he had no strength to rally, and so died, leaving Sara with no one to take care of her.

Miss Minchin's cold and fishy eyes had never looked so cold and fishy as they did when Sara went into the parlor, on being sent for, a few days after the letter was received.

No one had said anything to the child about mourning, so, in her old-fashioned way, she had decided to find a black dress for herself, and had picked out a black velvet she had outgrown and came into the room in it, looking the queerest little figure in the world, and a sad little figure too. The dress was too short and too tight, her face was white, her eyes had dark rings around them, and her doll, wrapped in a piece of old black crepe, was held under her arm. She was not a pretty child. She was thin, and had a weird, interesting little face, short black hair, and very large, green-gray eyes fringed all around with heavy black lashes.

"I am the ugliest child in the school," she had said once, after staring at herself in the glass for some minutes.

But there had been a clever, good-natured little French teacher who had said to the music master:

"Zat leetle Crewe child! A so ogly beauty! Ze so large eyes! Ze so spirituelle leetle face. Waid till she grow up. You shall see!"

This morning, however, in the tight, small black frock, she looked thinner and odder than ever, and her eyes were fixed on Miss Minchin with a queer steadiness as she slowly advanced into the parlor, clutching her doll.

"Put your doll down!" said Miss Minchin.

"No," said the child, "I won't put her down; I want her with me. She is all I have. She has stayed with me all the time since my papa died."

She had never been an obedient child. She had had her own way ever since she was born, and there was about her an air of silent determination under which Miss Minchin had always felt secretly uncomfortable. And that lady felt even now that perhaps it would be as well not to insist on her point. So she looked at her as severely as possible.

"You will have no time for dolls in future," she said. "You will have to work and improve yourself, and make yourself useful." Sara kept the big odd eyes fixed on her teacher and said nothing.

"Everything will be very different now," Miss Minchin went on. "I sent for you to talk to you and make you understand. Your father is dead. You have no friends. You have no money. You have no home and no one to take care of you."

The little pale-olive face twitched nervously, but the green-gray eyes did not move from Miss Minchin's, and still Sara said nothing.

"What are you staring at?" demanded Miss Minchin sharply. "Are you so stupid you don't understand what I mean? I tell you that you are quite alone in the world and have no one to do anything for you, unless I choose to keep you here."

The truth was, Miss Minchin was in her worst mood. To be suddenly deprived of a large sum of money yearly and of a show pupil, and to find herself with a little beggar on her hands, was more than she could bear with any degree of calmness.

"Now listen to me," she went on, "and remember what I say. If you work hard and prepare to make yourself useful in a few years, I shall let you stay here. You are only a child, but you are a sharp child, and you pick up things almost without being taught. You speak French very well, and in a year or so you can begin to help with the younger pupils. By the time you are fifteen you ought to be able to do that much at least."

"I can speak French better than you now," said Sara; "I always spoke it with my papa in India." Which was not at all polite, but was painfully true; because Miss Minchin could not speak French at all, and indeed was not in the least a clever person. But she was a hard, grasping businesswoman, and after the first shock of disappointment had seen that, at very little expense to herself, she might prepare this clever, determined child to be very useful to her and save her the necessity of paying large salaries to teachers of languages.

"Don't be impudent, or you will be punished," she said. "You will have to improve your manners if you expect to earn your bread. You are not a parlor boarder now. Remember that if you don't please me and I send you away, you have no home but the street. You can go now."

Sara turned away.

"Stay," commanded Miss Minchin, "don't you intend to thank me?"

Sara turned toward her. The nervous twitch was to

be seen again in her face, and she seemed to be trying to control it.

"What for?" she said.

"For my kindness to you," replied Miss Minchin. "For my kindness in giving you a home."

Sara went two or three steps nearer to her. Her thin little chest was heaving up and down, and she spoke in a strange, unchildish voice.

"You are not kind," she said. "You are not kind." And she turned again and went out of the room, leaving Miss Minchin staring after her strange, small figure in stony anger.

The child walked up the staircase, holding tightly to her doll; she meant to go to her bedroom, but at the door she was met by Miss Amelia.

"You are not to go in there," she said. "That is not your room now."

"Where is my room?" asked Sara.

"You are to sleep in the attic, next to the cook."

Sara walked on. She mounted two flights more and reached the door of the attic room, opened it, and went in, shutting it behind her. She stood against it and looked about her. The room was slanting-roofed and whitewashed; there was a rusty grate, an iron bedstead, and some odd articles of furniture sent up from better rooms below, where they had been used until they were considered to be worn out. Under the sky-light in the roof, which showed nothing but an oblong piece of dull-gray sky, there was a battered old red footstool.

Sara went to it and sat down. She was a queer child, as I have said before, and quite unlike other children. She seldom cried. She did not cry now. She laid her doll, Emily, across her knees, put her face down upon the doll and her arms around her, and sat there, her little black head resting on the black crepe, not saying one word, not making one sound.

A
Princess
in
Rags

From that day her life changed entirely. Sometimes she used to feel as if it must be another life altogether — the life of some other child. She was a little drudge and outcast; she was given her lessons at odd times, and expected to learn without being taught; she was sent on errands by Miss Minchin, Miss Amelia, and the cook. Nobody took any notice of her except when they ordered her about. She was often kept busy all day, and then sent into the deserted schoolroom with a pile of books to learn her lessons or practice at night. She had never been intimate with the other pupils, and soon she became so shabby that, taking her queer clothes together with her queer little ways, they began to look upon her as a being of another world than their own. The fact was that, as a rule, Miss

Minchin's pupils were rather dull, matter-of-fact young people, accustomed to being rich and comfortable; and Sara, with her elfish cleverness, her desolate life, and her odd habit of fixing her eyes upon them and staring them out of countenance, was too much for them.

"She always looks as if she were finding you out," said one girl, who was sly and given to making mischief.

"I am," said Sara promptly, when she heard of it. "That's what I look at them for. I like to know about people. I think them over afterward."

She never made any mischief herself or interfered with anyone. She talked very little, did as she was told, and thought a great deal. Nobody knew, and in fact nobody cared, whether she was unhappy or happy, unless perhaps it was Emily, who lived in the attic and slept on the iron bedstead at night. Sara thought Emily understood her feelings, though she was only wax and had a habit of staring herself. Sara used to talk to her at night.

"You are the only friend I have in the world," she would say to her. "Why don't you say something? Why don't you speak? Sometimes I am sure you could, if you would try. It ought to make you try, to know you are the only thing I have. If I were you, I should try. Why don't you try?"

It really was a very strange feeling she had about Emily. It arose from her being so desolate. She did not like to own to herself that her only friend, her only companion, could feel and hear nothing. She wanted to believe, or pretend to believe, that Emily understood and sympathized with her — that she heard her, even though she did not speak in answer. She used to put her in a chair sometimes and sit opposite her on the old red footstool and stare at her, and think and pretend about her until her own eyes would grow large with something which was almost like fear — particularly at night, when the garret was so still, when the only sound to be heard was the occasional squeak and scurry of rats in the wainscot. There were rat holes in the garret, and Sara detested rats, and was always glad Emily was with her when she heard their hateful squeak and rush and scratching. One of her "pretends" was that Emily was a kind of good witch and could protect her. Poor little Sara! Everything was "pretend" with her. She had a strong imagination; there was almost more imagination than there was Sara, and her whole forlorn, uncared-for child life was made up of imaginings. She imagined and pretended things until she almost believed them, and she would scarcely have been surprised at any remarkable thing that could have happened. So she insisted to herself that Emily understood all about her troubles and was really her friend.

"As to answering," she used to say, "I don't answer very often. I never answer when I can help it. When people are insulting you, there is nothing so good for them as not to say a word — just to look at them and *think*. Miss Minchin turns pale with rage when I do it. Miss Amelia looks frightened; so do the girls. They know you are stronger than they are, because you are strong enough to hold in your rage and they are not, and they say stupid things they wish they hadn't said afterward. There's nothing so strong as rage, except what makes you hold it in — that's stronger. It's a good thing not to answer your enemies. I scarcely ever do. Perhaps Emily is more like me than I am like myself. Perhaps she would rather not answer her friends even. She keeps it all in her heart."

But though she tried to satisfy herself with these arguments, Sara did not find it easy. When, after a long, hard day, in which she had been sent here and there, sometimes on long errands, through wind and cold and rain; and, when she came in wet and hungry, had been sent out again because nobody chose to remember that she was only a child, and that her thin little legs might be tired and her small body, clad in its forlorn, too small finery, all too short and too tight, might be chilled; when she had been given only harsh words and cold, slighting looks for thanks; when the cook had been vulgar and insolent; when Miss Minchin had been in her worst moods, and when she had seen the girls sneering at her among themselves and making fun of her poor, outgrown clothes — then Sara did not find Emily quite all that her sore, proud, desolate little heart needed as the doll sat in her old chair and stared.

One of these nights, when she came up to the garret cold, hungry, tired, and with a tempest raging in her small breast, Emily's stare seemed so vacant, her sawdust legs and arms so limp and inexpressive, that Sara lost all control over herself.

"I shall die presently!" she said at first.

Emily stared.

"I can't bear this!" said the poor child, trembling. "I know I shall die. I'm cold, I'm wet, I'm starving to death. I've walked a thousand miles today, and they have done nothing but scold me from morning until night. And because I could not find that last thing they sent me for, they would not give me any supper. Some men laughed at me because my old shoes made me slip down in the mud. I'm covered with mud now. And they laughed! Do you *hear!*"

She looked at the staring glass eyes and complacent wax face, and suddenly a sort of heartbroken rage seized her. She lifted her little savage hand and knocked Emily off the chair, bursting into a passion of sobbing.

"You are nothing but a doll!" she cried. "Nothing but a doll — doll — doll! You care for nothing. You are stuffed with sawdust. You never had a heart. Nothing could ever make you feel. You are a *doll!*"

Emily lay upon the floor, with her legs ignominiously doubled up over her head and a new flat place on the end of her nose, but she was still calm — even dignified.

Sara hid her face on her arms and sobbed. Some rats in the wall began to fight and bite each other, and squeak and scramble. But, as I have already intimated, Sara was not in the habit of crying. After a while she stopped, and when she stopped she looked at Emily, who seemed to be gazing at her around the side of one ankle, and actually with a kind of glassy-eyed sympathy. Sara bent and picked her up. Remorse overtook her.

"You can't help being a doll," she said, with a resigned sigh, "any more than those girls downstairs can help not having any sense. We are not all alike. Perhaps you do your sawdust best."

None of Miss Minchin's young ladies was very remarkable for being brilliant; they were select, but some of them were very dull, and some of them were not fond of applying themselves to their lessons. Sara, who snatched her lessons at all sorts of untimely hours from tattered and discarded books, and who had a hungry craving for everything readable, was often severe with them in her small mind. They had books they never read; she had no books at all. If she had always had something to read, she would not have been so lonely.

She liked romances and history and poetry; she would read anything. There was a sentimental housemaid in the establishment who bought the weekly penny papers and subscribed to a circulating library, from which she got greasy volumes containing stories of marquises and dukes who invariably fell in love with orange girls and gypsies and servantmaids, and made them the proud brides of coronets; and Sara often did parts of this maid's work so that she might earn the privilege of reading these romantic histories. There was also a fat, dull pupil, whose name was Ermengarde St. John, who was one of her resources. Ermengarde had an intellectual father, who, in his despairing desire to encourage his daughter, constantly sent her valuable and interesting books, which were a continual source of grief to her. Sara had once actually found her crying over a big package of them.

"What is the matter with you?" she asked her, perhaps rather disdainfully.

And it is just possible she would not have spoken to her if she had not seen the books. The sight of books always gave Sara a hungry feeling, and she could not help drawing near to them, if only to read their titles.

"What is the matter with you?" she asked.

"My papa has sent me some more books," answered Ermengarde woefully, "and expects me to read them."

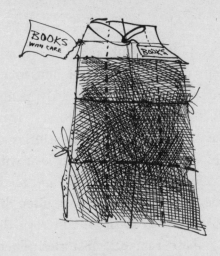

"Don't you like reading?" said Sara.

"I hate it!" replied Miss Ermengarde St. John. "And he will ask me questions when he sees me; he will want to know how much I remember. How would *you* like to have to read all those?"

"I'd like it better than anything else in the world," said Sara.

Ermengarde wiped her eyes to look at such a prodigy.

"Oh, gracious!" she exclaimed.

Sara returned the look with interest. A sudden plan formed itself in her sharp mind.

"Look here!" she said. "If you'll lend me those books, I'll read them and tell you everything that's in them afterward, and I'll tell it to you so that you will remember it. I know I can. The A B C children always remember what I tell them."

"Oh, goodness!" said Ermengarde. "Do you think you could?"

"I know I could," answered Sara. "I like to read, and I always remember. I'll take care of the books, too; they will look just as new as they do now when I give them back to you."

Ermengarde put her handkerchief in her pocket.

"If you'll do that," she said, "and if you'll make me remember, I'll give you — I'll give you some money."

"I don't want your money," said Sara. "I want your books — I want them." And her eyes grew big and queer, and her chest heaved once.

"Take them, then," said Ermengarde. "I wish I wanted them, but I am not clever and my father is, and he thinks I ought to be."

Sara picked up the books and marched off with them. But when she was at the door, she stopped and turned around.

"What are you going to tell your father?" she asked.

"Oh," said Ermengarde, "he needn't know; he'll think I've read them."

Sara looked down at the books; her heart really began to beat fast.

"I won't do it," she said rather slowly, "if you are going to tell him lies about it. I don't like lies. Why can't you tell him I read them and then told you about them?"

"But he wants *me* to read them," said Ermengarde.

"He wants you to know what is in them," said Sara; "and if I can tell it to you in an easy way and make you remember, I should think he would like that."

"He would like it better if I read them myself," replied Ermengarde.

"He will like it, I daresay, if you learn anything in any way," said Sara. "I should, if I were your father."

And though this was not a flattering way of stating the case, Ermengarde was obliged to admit it was true and, after a little more argument, gave in. And afterward she always used to hand over her books to Sara, and Sara would carry them to her garret and devour them; and after she had read each volume, she would return it and tell Ermengarde about it in a way of her own. She had a gift for making things interesting. Her imagination helped her to make everything rather like a story, and she managed to do this so well that Miss St. John gained more information from her books than she would have gained if she had read them three times over by her poor stupid little self. When Sara sat down by her and began to tell some story of travel or history, she made the travelers and historical people seem real; and Ermengarde used to sit and regard her dramatic gesticulations, her thin little flushed cheeks, and her shining, odd eyes with amazement.

"It sounds nicer than it seems in the book," she would say. "I never cared about Mary, Queen of Scots, before, and I always hated the French Revolution, but you make it seem like a story."

"It *is* a story," Sara would answer. "They are all stories. Everything is a story — everything in this world. You are a story — I am a story — Miss Minchin is a story. You can make a story out of anything."

"*I* can't," said Ermengarde.

Sara stared at her a minute reflectively.

"No," she said at last. "I suppose you couldn't. You are a little like Emily."

"Who is Emily?"

Sara recollected herself. She knew she was sometimes rather impolite in the candor of her remarks, and she did not want to be impolite to a girl who was not unkind — only stupid. Notwithstanding all her sharp little ways, she had the sense to wish to be just to everybody. In the hours she spent alone, she used to argue out a great many curious questions with herself. One thing she had decided upon was that a person who was clever ought to be clever enough not to be unjust or deliberately unkind to anyone. Miss Minchin was unjust and cruel, Miss Amelia was unkind and spiteful, the cook was malicious and hasty-tempered — they all were stupid and made her despise them, and she desired to be as unlike them as possible. So she would be as polite as she could to people who in the least deserved politeness.

"Emily is — a person — I know," she replied.

"Do you like her?" asked Ermengarde.

"Yes, I do," said Sara.

Ermengarde examined her queer little face and figure again. She did look odd. She had on, that day, a faded blue plush skirt which barely covered her knees, a brown cloth sacque, and a pair of olive-green stockings which Miss Minchin had made her piece out with black ones, so that they would be long enough to be kept on. And yet Ermengarde was beginning slowly to admire her. Such a forlorn, thin, neglected little thing as that, who could read and read and remember and tell you things so that they did not tire you all out! A child who could speak French and who had learned German, no one knew how! One could not help staring at her and feeling interested, particularly one to whom the simplest lesson was a trouble and a woe.

"Do you like *me?*" said Ermengarde, finally, at the end of her scrutiny.

Sara hesitated one second, then she answered:

"I like you because you are not ill-natured — I like you for letting me read your books — I like you because you don't make spiteful fun of me for what I can't help. It's not your fault that —"

She pulled herself up quickly. She had been going to say, "that you are stupid."

"That what?" asked Ermengarde.

"That you can't learn things quickly. If you can't, you can't. If I can, why, I can — that's all." She paused a minute, looking at the plump face before her, and then, rather slowly, one of her wise, old-fashioned thoughts came to her.

"Perhaps," she said, "to be able to learn things quickly isn't everything. To be kind is worth a good deal to other people. If Miss Minchin knew everything on earth, which she doesn't, and if she was like what she is now, she'd still be a detestable thing and everybody would hate her. Lots of clever people have done harm and been wicked. Look at Robespierre —"

She stopped again and examined her companion's countenance.

"Do you remember about him?" she demanded. "I believe you've forgotten."

"Well, I don't remember *all* of it," admitted Ermengarde.

"Well," said Sara, with courage and determination, "I'll tell it to you over again."

And she plunged once more into the gory records of the French Revolution, and told such stories of it and made such vivid pictures of its horrors that Miss St. John was afraid to go to bed afterward, and hid her head under the blankets when she did go, and shivered until she fell asleep. But afterward she preserved lively recollections of the character of Robespierre, and did not even forget Marie Antoinette and the Princess de Lamballe.

"You know they put her head on a pike and danced around it," Sara had said, "and she had beautiful blonde hair; and when I think of her, I never see her head on her body, but always on a pike, with those furious people dancing and howling."

Yes, it was true; to this imaginative child everything was a story; and the more books she read, the more imaginative she became. One of her chief entertain-

ments was to sit in her garret, or walk about it, and "suppose" things. On a cold night, when she had not had enough to eat, she would draw the red footstool up before the empty grate, and say in the most intense voice:

"Suppose there was a wide steel grate here and a great glowing fire — a *glowing* fire — with beds of red-hot coal and lots of little dancing, flickering flames. Suppose there was a soft, deep rug, and this was a comfortable chair, all cushions and crimson velvet; and suppose I had on a crimson velvet frock and a deep lace collar, like a child in a picture; and suppose all the rest of the room was furnished in lovely colors, and there were bookshelves full of books, which changed by magic as soon as you had read them; and suppose there was a little table here, with a snow-white cover on it, and little silver dishes, and in one there was hot, hot soup, and in another a roast chicken, and in another some raspberry-jam tarts with criss-cross on them, and in another some grapes; and suppose Emily could speak, and we could sit and eat our supper, and then talk and read; and then suppose there was a soft, warm bed in the corner, and when we were tired we could go to sleep, and sleep as long as we liked."

Sometimes, after she had supposed things like these for half an hour, she would feel almost warm, and would creep into bed with Emily and fall asleep with a smile on her face.

"What large, downy pillows!" she would whisper. "What white sheets and fleecy blankets!" And she almost forgot that her real pillows had scarcely any feathers in them at all and smelled musty, and that her blankets and coverlid were thin and full of holes.

At another time she would "suppose" she was a princess, and then she would go about the house with an expression on her face which was a source of great secret annoyance to Miss Minchin, because it seemed as if the child scarcely heard the spiteful, insulting things said to her, or, if she heard them, did not care for them at all. Sometimes, while she was in the midst of some harsh and cruel speech, Miss Minchin would find the odd, unchildish eyes fixed upon her with something like a proud smile in them. At such times she did not know that Sara was saying to herself:

"You don't know that you are saying these things to a princess, and that if I chose I could wave my hand and order you to execution. I only spare you because I *am* a princess, and you are a poor, stupid, old, vulgar thing and don't know any better."

This used to please and amuse her more than anything else; and queer and fanciful as it was, she found
comfort in it, and it was not a bad thing for her. It
really kept her from being made rude and malicious
by the rudeness and malice of those about her.

"A princess must be polite," she said to herself. And
so when the servants, who took their tone from their
mistress, were insolent and ordered her about, she
would hold her head erect, and reply to them sometimes in a way which made them stare at her, it was so
quaintly civil.

"I am a princess in rags and tatters," she would
think, "but I am a princess, inside. It would be easy to
be a princess if I were dressed in cloth of gold; it is a
great deal more of a triumph to be one all the time
when no one knows it. There was Marie Antoinette:
when she was in prison and her throne was gone, and
she had only a black gown on and her hair was white,
and they insulted her and called her the Widow Capet,
she was a great deal more like a queen then than
when she was so gay and had everything grand. I like
her best then. Those howling mobs of people did not
frighten her. She was stronger than they were, even
when they cut her head off."

Once, when such thoughts were passing through her
mind, the look in her eyes so enraged 'Miss Minchin

that she flew at Sara and boxed her ears. Sara awakened from her dream, started a little, and then broke into a laugh.

"What are you laughing at, you bold, impudent child!" exclaimed Miss Minchin.

It took Sara a few seconds to remember she was a princess. Her cheeks were red and smarting from the blows she had received.

"I was thinking," she said.

"Beg my pardon immediately," said Miss Minchin.

"I will beg your pardon for laughing, if it was rude," said Sara; "but I won't beg your pardon for thinking."

"What were you thinking?" demanded Miss Minchin. "How dare you think? What were you thinking?"

This occurred in the schoolroom, and all the girls looked up from their books to listen. It always interested them when Miss Minchin flew at Sara, because Sara always said something queer and never seemed in the least frightened. She was not in the least frightened now, though her boxed ears were scarlet and her eyes were as bright as stars.

"I was thinking," she answered gravely and quite politely, "that you did not know what you were doing."

"That I did not know what I was doing!" Miss Minchin fairly gasped.

"Yes," said Sara, "and I was thinking what would happen if I were a princess and you boxed my ears — what I should do to you. And I was thinking that if I were one, you would never dare to do it, whatever I said or did. And I was thinking how surprised and frightened you would be if you suddenly found out —"

She had the imagined picture so clearly before her eyes that she spoke in a manner which had an effect even on Miss Minchin. It almost seemed for the moment to her narrow, unimaginative mind that there must be some real power behind this candid daring.

"What!" she exclaimed. "Found out what?"

"That I really was a princess," said Sara, "and could do anything — anything I liked."

"Go to your room," cried Miss Minchin breathlessly, "this instant. Leave the schoolroom — Attend to your lessons, young ladies."

Sara made a little bow.

"Excuse me for laughing, if it was impolite," she said, and walked out of the room, leaving Miss Minchin in a rage and the girls whispering over their books.

"I shouldn't be at all surprised if she did turn out to be something," said one of them. "Suppose she should!"

Six
Hot
Buns

THAT very afternoon Sara had an opportunity of
proving to herself whether she was really a princess
or not. It was a dreadful afternoon. For several days
it had rained continuously; the streets were chilly and
sloppy; there was mud everywhere — sticky London
mud — and over everything a pall of fog and drizzle.
Of course there were several long and tiresome errands

to be done — there always were on days like this — and Sara was sent out again and again, until her shabby clothes were damp through. The old feathers on her forlorn hat were more bedraggled and absurd than ever, and her downtrodden shoes were so wet they could not hold any more water. Added to this, she had been deprived of her dinner, because Miss Minchin wished to punish her. She was very hungry. She was so cold and hungry and tired that her little face had a pinched look, and now and then some kindhearted person passing her in the crowded street glanced at her with sympathy. But she did not know that. She hurried on, trying to comfort herself in that queer way of hers by pretending and "supposing"; but really this time it was harder than she had ever found it, and once or twice she thought it almost made her more cold and hungry instead of less so. But she persevered obstinately. "Suppose I had dry clothes on," she thought. "Suppose I had good shoes and a long, thick coat and merino stockings and a whole umbrella. And suppose — suppose, just when I was near a baker's where they sold hot buns, I should find sixpence which belonged to nobody. Suppose, if I did, I should go into the shop and buy six of the hottest buns, and should eat them all without stopping."

Some very odd things happen in this world sometimes. It certainly was an odd thing that happened
to Sara. She had to cross the street just as she was saying this to herself; the mud was dreadful — she almost
had to wade. She picked her way as carefully as she
could, but she could not save herself much; only in
picking her way she had to look down at her feet and
the mud, and in looking down — just as she reached the
pavement — she saw something shining in the gutter. A
piece of silver — a tiny piece trodden upon by many
feet, but still with spirit enough to shine a little. Not
quite a sixpence, but the next thing to it: a fourpenny
piece! In one second it was in her cold little red and
blue hand.

"Oh!" she gasped. "It is true!"

And then, if you will believe me, she looked straight
before her at the shop directly facing her. And it was
a baker's, and a cheerful, stout, motherly woman, with
rosy cheeks, was just putting into the window a tray of
delicious hot buns — large, plump, shiny buns, with
currants in them.

It almost made Sara feel faint for a few seconds —
the shock and the sight of the buns, and the delightful
odor of warm bread floating up through the baker's
cellar window.

She knew that she need not hesitate to use the little piece of money. It had evidently been lying in the mud for some time, and its owner was completely lost in the streams of passing people who crowded and jostled each other all through the day.

"But I'll go and ask the baker's woman if she has lost a piece of money," she said to herself, rather faintly.

So she crossed the pavement and put her wet foot on the step of the shop; and as she did so, she saw something which made her stop.

It was a little figure more forlorn than her own — a little figure which was not much more than a bundle of rags, from which small, bare, red, and muddy feet peeped out, only because the rags with which the wearer was trying to cover them were not long enough. Above the rags appeared a shock of tangled hair and a dirty face, with big, hollow, hungry eyes.

Sara knew they were hungry eyes the moment she saw them, and she felt a sudden sympathy.

"This," she said to herself, with a little sigh, "is one of the Populace — and she is hungrier than I am."

The child — this "one of the Populace" — stared up at Sara and shuffled herself aside a little, so as to give her more room. She was used to being made to give room to everybody. She knew that if a policeman chanced to see her, he would tell her to "move on."

Sara clutched her little fourpenny piece and hesitated a few seconds. Then she spoke to her.

"Are you hungry?" she asked.

The child shuffled herself and her rags a little more.

"Ain't I jist!" she said, in a hoarse voice. "Jist ain't I!"

"Haven't you had any dinner?" said Sara.

"No dinner," more hoarsely still and with more shuffling, "nor yet no bre'fast — nor yet no supper."

"Since when?" asked Sara

"Dun'no. Never got nothin' today — nowhere. I've axed and axed."

Just to look at her made Sara more hungry and faint. But those queer little thoughts were at work in her brain, and she was talking to herself though she was sick at heart.

"If I'm a princess," she was saying, "if I'm a princess — ! When they were poor and driven from their thrones, they always shared with the Populace if they met one poorer and hungrier. They always shared. Buns are a penny each. If it had been sixpence! I could have eaten six. It won't be enough for either of us, but it will be better than nothing."

"Wait a minute," she said to the beggar child. She went into the shop. It was warm and smelled delightful. The woman was just going to put more hot buns in the window.

"If you please," said Sara, "have you lost fourpence — a silver fourpence?" And she held the forlorn little piece of money out to her.

The woman looked at it and at her — at her intense little face and bedraggled, once-fine clothes.

"Bless us — no," she answered. "Did you find it?"

"In the gutter," said Sara.

"Keep it then," said the woman. "It may have been there a week, and goodness knows who lost it. *You* could never find out."

"I know that," said Sara, "but I thought I'd ask you."

"Not many would," said the woman, looking puzzled and interested and good-natured all at once. "Do you want to buy something?" she added, as she saw Sara glance toward the buns.

"Four buns, if you please," said Sara, "those at a penny each."

The woman went to the window and put some in a paper bag. Sara noticed that she put in six.

"I said four, if you please," she explained. "I have only the fourpence."

"I'll throw in two for good measure," said the woman pleasantly. "I daresay you can eat them sometime. Aren't you hungry?"

A mist rose before Sara's eyes.

"Yes," she answered. "I am very hungry, and I am much obliged to you for your kindness, and," she was going to add, "there is a child outside who is hungrier than I am." But just at that moment two or three customers came in at once, and each one seemed in a hurry, so she could only thank the woman again and go out.

The child was still huddled up on the corner of the steps. She looked frightful in her wet and dirty rags. She was staring with a stupid look of suffering straight before her, and Sara saw her suddenly draw the back of her roughened, black hand across her eyes to rub away the tears which seemed to have surprised her by forcing their way from under her lids. She was muttering to herself.

Sara opened the paper bag and took out one of the hot buns, which had already warmed her cold hands a little.

"See," she said, putting the bun on the ragged lap, "that is nice and hot. Eat it, and you will not be so hungry."

The child started and stared up at her; then she snatched up the bun and began to cram it into her mouth with great wolfish bites.

"Oh my! Oh my!" Sara heard her say hoarsely, in wild delight. *"Oh my!"*

Sara took out three more buns and put them down.

"She is hungrier than I am," she said to herself. "She's starving." But her hand trembled when she put down the fourth bun. "I'm not starving," she said, and she put down the fifth.

The little starving London savage was still snatching and devouring when Sara turned away. She was too ravenous to give any thanks, even if she had been taught politeness, which she had not. She was only a poor little wild animal.

"Good-by," said Sara.

When she reached the other side of the street, she looked back. The child had a bun in both hands, and had stopped in the middle of a bite to watch her. Sara gave her a little nod, and the child, after another stare — a curious, longing stare — jerked her shaggy head in response, and until Sara was out of sight she did not take another bite or even finish the one she had begun.

At that moment the baker woman glanced out of her shop window.

"Well, I never!" she exclaimed. "If that young 'un hasn't given her buns to a beggar child! It wasn't because she didn't want them, either — well, well, she looked hungry enough. I'd give something to know what she did it for." She stood behind her window for a few moments and pondered. Then her curiosity got the better of her. She went to the door and spoke to the beggar child.

"Who gave you those buns?" she asked her.

The child nodded her head toward Sara's vanishing figure.

"What did she say?" inquired the woman.

"Axed me if I was 'ungry," replied the hoarse voice.

"What did you say?"

"Said I was jist!"

"And then she came in and got buns and came out and gave them to you, did she?"

The child nodded.

"How many?"

"Five."

The woman thought it over. "Left just one for herself," she said in a low voice. "And she could have eaten the whole six — I saw it in her eyes."

She looked after the little bedraggled, faraway figure, and felt more disturbed in her usually comfortable mind than she had for many a day.

"I wish she hadn't gone so quick," she said. "I'm blest if she shouldn't have had a dozen."

Then she turned to the child.

"Are you hungry, yet?" she asked.

"I'm allus 'ungry," was the answer, "but 'tain't so bad as it was."

"Come in here," said the woman, and she held open the shop door.

The child got up and shuffled in. To be invited into a warm place full of bread seemed an incredible thing. She did not know what was going to happen; she did not care, even.

"Get yourself warm," said the woman, pointing to a fire in a tiny back room. "And, look here: when you're hard up for a bit of bread, you can come here and ask for it. I'm blest if I won't give it to you for that young un's sake."

Sara's Secret Friend

Sara found some comfort in her remaining bun. It was hot, and it was a great deal better than nothing. She broke off small pieces and ate them slowly, to make it last longer.

"Suppose it was a magic bun," she said, "and a bite was as much as a whole dinner. I should be overeating myself if I went on like this."

It was dark when she reached the square in which Miss Minchin's Select Seminary was situated; the lamps were lighted, and in most of the windows gleams of light were to be seen. It always interested Sara to catch glimpses of the rooms before the shutters were closed.

She liked to imagine things about people who sat before the fires in the houses, or who bent over books at the tables. There was, for instance, the Large Family opposite. She called these people the Large Family — not because they were large, for indeed most of them were little, but because there were so many of them. There were eight children in the Large Family, and a stout, rosy mother, and a stout, rosy father, and a stout, rosy grandmamma, and any number of servants. The eight children were always either being taken out to walk, or to ride in perambulators, by comfortable nurses; or they were going to drive with their mamma; or they were flying to the door in the evening to kiss their papa, and dance around him and drag off his overcoat and look for packages in the pockets of it; or they were crowding about the nursery windows and looking out and pushing each other and laughing — in fact, they were always doing something which seemed enjoyable and suited to the tastes of a large family. Sara was quite attached to them, and had given them all names out of books. She called them the Montmorencys, when she did not call them the Large Family. The fat, fair baby with the lace cap was Ethelberta Beauchamp Montmorency; the next baby was Violet Cholmondely Montmorency; the little boy who could just stagger, and who had such round legs, was Sydney Cecil Vivian Montmorency; and then came Lilian Evangeline, Guy Clarence, Maud Marian Rosalind, Gladys Veronica Eustacia, and Claude Harold Hector.

Next door to the Large Family lived the Maiden Lady, who had a companion and two parrots, and a King Charles spaniel; but Sara was not so very fond of her, because she did nothing in particular but talk to the parrots and drive out with the spaniel. The most interesting person of all lived next door to Miss Minchin herself. Sara called him the Indian Gentleman. He was an elderly gentleman who was said to have lived in the East Indies, and to be immensely rich and to have something the matter with his liver — in fact, it had been rumored that he had no liver at all, and was much inconvenienced by the fact. At any rate, he was very yellow and he did not look happy; and when he went out to his carriage, he was almost always wrapped up in shawls and overcoats, as if he were cold. He had a native servant who looked even colder than himself, and he had a monkey who looked colder than

the native servant. Sara had seen the monkey sitting on a table, in the sun, in the parlor window, and he always wore such a mournful expression that she sympathized with him deeply.

"I daresay," she used sometimes to remark to herself, "he is thinking all the time of coconut trees and of swinging by his tail under a tropical sun. He might have had a family dependent on him too, poor thing!"

The native servant, whom she called the Lascar,

looked mournful too, but he was evidently very faithful to his master.

"Perhaps he saved his master's life in the Sepoy rebellion," she thought. "They look as if they might have had all sorts of adventures. I wish I could speak to the Lascar. I remember a little Hindustani."

And one day she actually did speak to him, and his start at the sound of his own language expressed a great deal of surprise and delight. He was waiting for his master to come out to the carriage, and Sara, who was

going on an errand as usual, stopped and spoke a few words. She had a special gift for languages, and had remembered enough Hindustani to make herself understood by him. When his master came out, the Lascar spoke to him quickly, and the Indian Gentleman turned and looked at her curiously. And afterward the Lascar always greeted her with salaams of the most profound description. And occasionally they exchanged a few words. She learned that it was true that the Sahib was very rich, that he was ill, and also that he had no wife nor children and that England did not agree with the monkey.

"He must be as lonely as I am," thought Sara. "Being rich does not seem to make him happy."

That evening, as she passed the windows, the Lascar was closing the shutters, and she caught a glimpse of the room inside. There was a bright fire glowing in the grate, and the Indian Gentleman was sitting before it, in a luxurious chair. The room was richly furnished and looked delightfully comfortable, but the Indian Gentleman sat with his head resting on his hand, and looked as lonely and unhappy as ever.

"Poor man!" said Sara; "I wonder what *you* are supposing ?"

When she went into the house, she met Miss Minchin in the hall.

"Where have you been wasting your time?" said Miss Minchin. "You've been out for hours!"

"It was so wet and muddy," Sara answered. "It was hard to walk, because my shoes were so bad and slipped about so."

"Make no excuses," said Miss Minchin, "and tell no falsehoods."

Sara went downstairs to the kitchen.

"Why didn't you stay all night?" said the cook.

"Here are the things," said Sara, and laid her purchases on the table.

The cook looked over them, grumbling. She was in a very bad temper indeed.

"May I have something to eat?" Sara asked rather faintly.

"Tea's over and done with," was the answer. "Did you expect me to keep it hot for you?"

Sara was silent a second.

"I had no dinner," she said, and her voice was quite low. She made it low, because she was afraid it would tremble.

"There's some bread in the pantry," said the cook. "That's all you'll get at this time of day."

Sara went and found the bread. It was old and hard and dry. The cook was in too bad a humor to give her anything to eat with it. She had just been scolded by Miss Minchin, and it was always safe and easy to vent her own spite on Sara.

Really it was hard for the child to climb the three long flights of stairs leading to her garret. She often found them long and steep when she was tired, but tonight it seemed as if she would never reach the top. Several times a lump rose in her throat, and she was obliged to stop to rest.

"I can't pretend anything more tonight," she said wearily to herself. "I'm sure I can't. I'll eat my bread and drink some water and then go to sleep, and perhaps a dream will come and pretend for me. I wonder what dreams are."

Yes, when she reached the top landing there were tears in her eyes, and she did not feel like a princess — only like a tired, hungry, lonely child.

"If my papa had lived," she said, "they would not have treated me like this. If my papa had lived, he would have taken care of me."

Then she turned the handle and opened the garret door.

Can you imagine it — can you believe it? I find it hard to believe myself. And Sara found it impossible. For the first few moments she thought something strange had happened to her eyes — to her mind — that the dream had come before she had time to fall asleep.

"Oh!" she exclaimed breathlessly. "Oh! It isn't true! I know, I know it isn't true!" And she slipped into the room and closed the door and locked it, and stood with her back against it, staring straight before her.

Do you wonder? In the grate, which had been empty and rusty and cold when she left it, but which now was blackened and polished up quite respectably, there was a glowing, blazing fire. On the hob was a little brass kettle, hissing and boiling; spread upon the floor was a warm, thick rug; before the fire was a folding chair,

unfolded and with cushions on it; by the chair was a small folding table, unfolded, covered with a white cloth, and upon it were spread small covered dishes, a cup and saucer, and a teapot; on the bed were new,

warm coverings, a curious wadded silk robe, and some books. The little, cold, miserable room seemed changed into fairyland. It was actually warm and glowing.

"It is bewitched!" said Sara. " Or *I* am bewitched. I only *think* I see it all; but if I can only keep on thinking it, I don't care — I don't care — if only I can keep it up!"

She was afraid to move, for fear it would melt away. She stood with her back against the door and looked and looked. But soon she began to feel warm, and then she moved forward.

"A fire that I only *thought* I saw surely wouldn't *feel* warm," she said. "It feels real — real."

She went to it and knelt before it. She touched the chair, the table; she lifted the cover of one of the dishes. There was something hot and savory in it — something delicious. The teapot had tea in it, ready for the boiling water from the little kettle; one plate had toast on it, another, muffins.

"It is real," said Sara. "The fire is real enough to warm me; I can sit in the chair; the things are real enough to eat."

It was like a fairy story come true — it was heavenly. She went to the bed and touched the blankets and the wrap. They were real, too. She opened one book, and on the title page was written in a strange hand, "To the Little Girl in the Attic."

Suddenly — was it a strange thing for her to do? — Sara put her face down on the queer, foreign-looking quilted robe and burst into tears.

"I don't know who it is," she said, "but somebody cares about me a little — somebody is my friend."

Somehow that thought warmed her more than the fire. She had never had a friend since those happy, luxurious days when she had had everything; and those days had seemed such a long way off — so far away as to be only like dreams — during these last years at Miss Minchin's.

She really cried more at this strange thought of having a friend, even though an unknown one, than she had cried over many of her worst troubles. But these tears seemed different from the others, for when she had wiped them away they did not seem to leave her eyes and her heart hot and smarting.

And then imagine, if you can, what the rest of the evening was like. The delicious comfort of taking off the damp clothes and putting on the soft, warm, quilted robe before the glowing fire, of slipping her cold feet into the luscious little wool-lined slippers she found near her chair. And then the hot tea and savory dishes, the cushioned chair and the books!

It was just like Sara that, once having found the things real, she should give herself up to the enjoyment of them to the very utmost. She had lived such a life of imagining, and had found her pleasure so long in improbabilities, that she was quite equal to accepting any wonderful thing that happened. After she was quite warm, and had eaten her supper and enjoyed herself for an hour or so, it had almost ceased to be surprising to her that such magical surroundings should be hers. As to finding out who had done all this, she knew that it was out of the question. She did not know a human soul by whom it could seem in the least degree probable that it could have been done.

"There is nobody," she said to herself, "nobody." She discussed the matter with Emily, it is true, but more because it was delightful to talk about it than with a view to making any discoveries.

"But we have a friend, Emily," she said; "we have a friend."

The Indian
Gentleman
and His
Monkey

Sara could not even imagine a being charming
enough to fill her grand ideal of her mysterious bene-
factor. If she tried to make in her mind a picture of
him or her, it ended by being something glittering and
strange — not at all like a real person, but bearing
resemblance to a sort of Eastern magician, with long
robes and a wand. And when she fell asleep beneath
the soft white blanket, she dreamed all night of this
magnificent personage, and talked to him in Hindustani, and made salaams to him.

Upon one thing she was determined: she would not speak to anyone of her good fortune; it should be her own secret. In fact, she was rather inclined to think that if Miss Minchin knew, she would take her treasures from her or in some way spoil her pleasure. So when she went down the next morning, she shut her door very tight and did her best to look as if nothing unusual had occurred. And yet this was rather hard, because she could not help remembering every now and then, with a sort of start, and her heart would beat quickly every time she repeated to herself, "I have a friend!"

It was a friend who evidently meant to continue to be kind, for when she went to her garret the next night — and she opened the door, it must be confessed, with rather an excited feeling — she found that the same hands had been again at work and had done even more than before. The fire and the supper were again there, and beside them a number of other things which so altered the look of the garret that Sara quite lost her breath. A piece of bright, strange, heavy cloth covered the battered mantel, and on it some ornaments had been placed. All the bare, ugly things which could be covered with draperies had been concealed and made to look quite pretty. Some odd materials in rich colors had been fastened against the walls with fine, sharp tacks — so sharp that they could be pressed into the wood without hammering. Some brilliant fans were pinned up, and there were several large cushions. A long, old wooden box was covered with a rug, and some cushions lay on it, so that it wore quite the air of a sofa.

Sara simply sat down and looked, and looked again.

"It is exactly like a fairy story come true," she said; "there isn't the least difference. I feel as if I might wish for anything — diamonds and bags of gold — and they would appear! *That* couldn't be any stranger than this. Is this my garret? Am I the same cold, ragged, damp Sara? And to think how I used to pretend and pretend, and wish there were fairies! The one thing I always wanted was to see a fairy story come true. I am *living* in a fairy story! I feel as if I might be a fairy my-self, and be able to turn things into anything else!"

It was like a fairy story, and, what was best of all, it continued. Almost every day something new was done to the garret. Some new comfort or ornament appeared in it when Sara open her door at night, until actually, in a short time, it was a bright little room, full of all sorts of odd and luxurious things. And the magician had taken care that the child should not be hungry, and that she should have as many books as she could read. When she left the room in the morning, the remains of her supper were on the table; and when she returned in the evening, the magician had removed them and left another nice little meal. Downstairs Miss Minchin was as cruel and insulting as ever, Miss Amelia was as peevish, and the servants were as vulgar. Sara was sent on errands, and scolded, and driven hither and thither, but somehow it seemed as if she could bear it all. The delightful sense of romance and mystery lifted her above the cook's temper and malice. The comfort she enjoyed and could always look forward to was making her stronger. If she came home from her errands wet and tired, she knew she would soon be warm, after she had climbed the stairs. In a few weeks she began to look less thin. A little color came into her cheeks, and her eyes did not seem much too big for her face.

It was just when this was beginning to be so apparent that Miss Minchin sometimes stared at her questioningly, that another wonderful thing happened. A man came to the door and left several parcels. All were addressed (in large letters) to "The Little Girl in the Attic." Sara herself was sent to open the door, and she took them in. She laid the two largest parcels down on the hall table, and was looking at the address when Miss Minchin came down the stairs.

"Take the things upstairs to the young lady to whom

they belong," she said. "Don't stand there staring at them."

"They belong to me," answered Sara, quietly.

"To *you*!" exclaimed Miss Minchin. "What do you mean?"

"I don't know where they come from," said Sara, "but they're addressed to me."

Miss Minchin came to her side and looked at them with an excited expression.

"What is in them?" she demanded.

"I don't know," said Sara.

"Open them!" she demanded, still more excitedly.

Sara did as she was told. They contained pretty and comfortable clothing — clothing of different kinds: shoes and stockings and gloves, a warm coat, and even an umbrella. On the pocket of the coat was pinned a paper on which was written, "To be worn every day — will be replaced by others when necessary."

Miss Minchin was quite agitated. This was an incident which suggested strange things to her sordid mind. Could it be that she had made a mistake after all, and that the child so neglected and so unkindly treated by her had some powerful friend in the background? It would not be very pleasant if there should be such a friend and he or she should learn the truth about the thin, shabby clothes, the scant food, the hard work. She felt very queer indeed and uncertain, and she gave a side glance at Sara.

"Well," she said, in a voice such as she had never used since the day the child lost her father, "well, someone is very kind to you. As you have the things and are to have new ones when they are worn out, you may as well go and put them on and look respectable; and after you are dressed, you may come downstairs and learn your lessons in the schoolroom."

So it happened that, about half an hour afterward, Sara struck the entire schoolroom of pupils dumb with amazement by making her appearance in a costume such as she had never worn since the change of fortune whereby she ceased to be a show pupil and a parlor boarder. She scarcely seemed to be the same Sara. She was neatly dressed in a pretty gown of warm browns and reds, and even her stockings and slippers were nice and dainty.

"Perhaps someone has left her a fortune," one of the girls whispered. "I always thought something would happen to her, she is so queer."

That night when Sara went to her room she carried out a plan she had been devising for some time. She wrote a note to her unknown friend. It ran as follows:

I hope you will not think it is not polite that I should write this note to you when you wish to keep yourself a secret, but I do not mean to be impolite or to try to find out at all; only I want to thank you for being so kind to me — so beautiful kind — and making everything like a fairy story. I am so grateful to you, and I am so happy! I used to be so lonely and cold and hungry, and now, oh, just think what you have done for me! Please let me say just these words. It seems as if I ought to say them. *Thank you — thank you — thank you!*

THE LITTLE GIRL IN THE ATTIC

The next morning she left this on the little table, and it was taken away with the other things; so she felt sure the magician had received it, and she was happier for the thought.

A few nights later a very odd thing happened. She found something in the room which she certainly would never have expected. When she came in as usual, she saw something small and dark in her chair — an odd, tiny figure which turned toward her a weird-looking wistful little face.

"Why, it's the monkey!" she cried. "It is the Indian Gentleman's monkey! Where can he have come from?"

It *was* the monkey, sitting up and looking so like a mite of a child that it really was quite pathetic; and very soon Sara found out how he happened to be in her room. The skylight was open, and it was easy to guess that he had crept out of his master's garret window, which was only a few feet away and perfectly easy to get in and out of, even for a climber less agile than a monkey. He had probably climbed to the garret on a tour of investigation and, getting out upon the roof and being attracted by the light in Sara's attic, had crept in. At all events this seemed quite reasonable, and there he was; and when Sara went to him, he actually put out his queer, elfish little hands, caught her dress, and jumped into her arms.

"Oh, you queer, poor, ugly, strange little thing!" said
Sara, caressing him. "I can't help liking you. You look
like a sort of baby, but I am so glad you are not, because
your mother could *not* be proud of you, and nobody
would dare to say you were like any of your relations.
But I do like you; you have such a forlorn look in your

little face. Perhaps you are sorry you are so ugly, and it's always on your mind. I wonder if you have a mind?"

The monkey sat and looked at her while she talked, and seemed much interested in her remarks, if one could judge by his eyes and his forehead, and by the way he moved his head up and down and held it sideways and scratched it with his little hand. He examined Sara quite seriously, and anxiously too. He felt the stuff of her dress, touched her hands, climbed up and examined her ears, and then sat on her shoulder, holding a lock of her hair and looking mournful but not at all agitated. Upon the whole, he seemed pleased with Sara.

"But I must take you back," she said to him, "though I'm sorry to have to do it. Oh, the company you *would* be to a person!"

She lifted him from her shoulder, set him on her knee, and gave him a bit of cake. He sat and nibbled it, and then put his head on one side, looked at her, wrinkled his forehead, and then nibbled again, in the most companionable manner.

"But you must go home," said Sara at last; and she took him in her arms to carry him downstairs. Evidently he did not want to leave the room, for as they reached the door he clung to her neck and gave a little scream of anger.

"You mustn't be an ungrateful monkey," said Sara. "You ought to be fondest of your own family. I am sure the Lascar is good to you."

Nobody saw her go out, and very soon she was standing on the Indian Gentleman's front steps, and the Lascar had opened the door for her.

"I found your monkey in my room," she said in Hindustani. "I think he got in through the window."

The man began a rapid outpouring of thanks; but just as he was in the midst of them, a fretful, hollow voice was heard through the open door of the nearest room. The instant he heard it the Lascar disappeared, and left Sara still holding the monkey.

It was not many moments, however, before he came back bringing a message. His master had told him to bring Missy into the library. The Sahib was very ill, but he wished to see Missy.

Sara thought this odd, but she remembered reading stories of Indian gentlemen who, having no constitutions, were extremely cross and full of whims, and who must have their own way. So she followed the Lascar.

When she entered the room, the Indian Gentleman was lying on an easy chair, propped up with pillows. He looked frightfully ill. His yellow face was thin, and his eyes were hollow. He gave Sara a rather curious look — it was as if she awakened in him some anxious interest.

"You live next door?" he said.

"Yes," answered Sara. "I live at Miss Minchin's."

"She keeps a boarding school?"

"Yes," said Sara.

"And you are one of her pupils?"

Sara hesitated a moment.

"I don't know exactly what I am," she replied.

"Why not?" asked the Indian Gentleman.

The monkey gave a tiny squeak, and Sara stroked him.

"At first," she said, "I was a pupil and a parlor boarder, but now —"

"What do you mean by 'at first'?" asked the Indian Gentleman.

"When I was first taken there by my papa."

"Well, what has happened since then?" said the invalid, staring at her and knitting his brows with a puzzled expression.

"My papa died," said Sara. "He lost all his money, and there was none left for me — and there was no one to take care of me or pay Miss Minchin, so —"

"So you were sent up into the garret and neglected, and made into a half-starved little drudge!" put in the Indian Gentleman. "That's about it, isn't it?"

The color deepened on Sara's cheeks.

"There was no one to take care of me, and no money," she said. "I belong to nobody."

"What did your father mean by losing his money?" said the gentleman, fretfully.

The red in Sara's cheeks grew deeper, and she fixed her odd eyes on the yellow face.

"He did not lose it himself," she said. "He had a friend he was fond of, and it was his friend who took his money. I don't know how. I don't understand. He trusted his friend too much."

She saw the invalid start — the strangest start — as if he had been suddenly frightened. Then he spoke nervously and excitedly:

"That's an old story," he said. "It happens every day; but sometimes those who are blamed — those who do the wrong — don't intend it, and are not so bad. It may happen through a mistake — a miscalculation; they may not be so bad."

"No," said Sara, "but the suffering is just as bad for the others. It killed my papa."

The Indian Gentleman pushed aside some of the gorgeous wraps that covered him.

"Come a little nearer and let me look at you," he said.

His voice sounded very strange; it had a more nervous and excited tone than before. Sara had an odd fancy that he was half afraid to look at her. She came and stood nearer, the monkey clinging to her and watching his master anxiously over his shoulder.

The Indian Gentleman's hollow, restless eyes fixed themselves on her.

"Yes," he said at last. "Yes; I can see it. Tell me your father's name."

"His name was Ralph Crewe," said Sara. "Captain Crewe. Perhaps" — a sudden thought flashing upon her — "perhaps you may have heard of him? He died in India."

The Princess Sara

THE Indian Gentleman sank back upon his pillows. He looked very weak, and seemed out of breath.

"Yes," he said, "I knew him. I was his friend. I meant no harm. If he had only lived, he would have known. It turned out well after all. He was a fine young fellow. I was fond of him. I will make it right. Call — call the man."

Sara thought he was going to die. But there was no need to call the Lascar. He must have been waiting at the door. He was in the room and by his master's side in an instant. He seemed to know what to do. He lifted the drooping head and gave the invalid something in a small glass. The Indian Gentleman lay panting for a few minutes, and then he spoke in an exhausted but eager voice, addressing the Lascar in Hindustani:

"Go for Carmichael," he said. "Tell him to come here at once. Tell him I have found the child!"

When Mr. Carmichael arrived (which occurred in a very few minutes, for it turned out that he was none other than the father of the Large Family across the street), Sara went home and was allowed to take the monkey with her. She certainly did not sleep very much that night, though the monkey behaved beautifully and did not disturb her in the least. It was not the monkey that kept her awake — it was her thoughts, and her wonder as to what the Indian Gentleman had meant when he said, "Tell him I have found the child."

"What child?" Sara kept asking herself. "I was the only child there; but how had he found me, and why did he want to find me? And what is he going to do, now I am found? Is it something about my papa? Do I belong to somebody? Is he one of my relations? Is something going to happen?"

But she found out the very next day, in the morning; and it seemed that she had been living in a story even more than she had imagined. First Mr. Carmichael came and had an interview with Miss Minchin. And it appeared that Mr. Carmichael, besides occupying the important situation of father to the Large Family, was a lawyer and had charge of the affairs of Mr. Carrisford — which was the real name of the Indian Gentleman —

and, as Mr. Carrisford's lawyer, Mr. Carmichael had come to explain something curious to Miss Minchin regarding Sara. But being the father of the Large Family, he had a very kind and fatherly feeling for children; and so, after seeing Miss Minchin alone, what did he do but go and bring across the square his rosy, motherly, warmhearted wife, so that she herself might talk to the lonely little girl and tell her everything in the best and most motherly way.

And then Sara learned that she was to be a poor little drudge and outcast no more, and that a great change had come in her fortunes; for all the lost fortune had come back to her, and a great deal had even been added to it. It was Mr. Carrisford who had been her father's friend, and who had made the investments which had caused him the apparent loss of his money; but it had so happened that, after poor young Captain Crewe's death, one of the investments which had seemed at the time the very worst had taken a sudden turn and proved to be such a success that it had been a mine of wealth, and had more than doubled the Captain's lost fortune as well as making a fortune for Mr. Carrisford himself. But Mr. Carrisford had been very unhappy. He had truly loved his poor, handsome, generous young friend, and the knowledge that he had caused his death had weighed upon him always, and broken both his health and spirit. The worst of it had been that, when first he thought himself and Captain Crewe ruined, he had lost courage and gone away because he was not brave enough to face the consequences of what he had done, and so he had not even known where the young soldier's little girl had been placed. When he wanted to find her and make restitution, he could discover no trace of her; and the certainty that she was poor and friendless somewhere had made him more miserable than ever. When he had taken the house next to Miss Minchin's, he had been so ill and wretched that he had given up the search.

His troubles and the Indian climate had brought him almost to death's door; indeed, he had not been expected to live more than a few months. And then one day the Lascar had told him about Sara's speaking Hindustani, and gradually he had begun to take a sort of interest in the forlorn child, though he had only caught a glimpse of her once or twice and had not connected her with the child of his friend — perhaps because he was too languid to think much about anything. But the Lascar had found out something of Sara's unhappy little life, and about the garret. One evening he had actually crept out of his own garret window and looked into hers — which was a very easy matter, because, as I have said, it was only a few feet away — and he had told his master what he had seen, and in a moment of compassion the Indian Gentleman told him to take into the wretched little room such comforts as he could carry from the one window to the other. And the Lascar, who had developed an interest in and an odd fondness for the child who had spoken to him in his own tongue, had been pleased with the work; and having the silent swiftness and agile movements of many of his race, he had made his evening journeys across the few feet of roof from garret window to garret window without any trouble at all. He had watched Sara's movements until he knew exactly when she was absent from her room and when she returned to it, and so he had been able to calculate the best times for his work. Generally he made his trips in the dusk of the evening; but once or twice, when he had seen her go out on errands, he had dared to go over in the daytime, being quite sure that the garret was never entered by anyone but herself. His pleasure in the work and his reports of the results had added to the invalid's interest in it, and sometimes the master had found the planning gave him something to think of, which made him almost forget his weariness and pain. And at last, when Sara brought home the truant monkey, he had felt a wish to see her, and then her likeness to her father had done the rest.

"And now, my dear," said good Mrs. Carmichael,

patting Sara's hand, "all your troubles are over, I am sure, and you are to come home with me and be taken care of as if you were one of my own little girls; and we are so pleased to think of having you with us until everything is settled and Mr. Carrisford is better. The excitement of last night has made him very weak, but we really think he will get well, now that such a load is taken from his mind. And when he is stronger, I am sure he will be as kind to you as your own papa would have been. He has a very good heart, and he is fond of children — and he has no family at all. But we must make you happy and rosy, and you must learn to play and run about, as my little girls do —"

"As your little girls do?" said Sara. "I wonder if I could. I used to watch them and wonder what it was like. Shall I feel as if I belonged to somebody?"

"Ah, my love, yes! — yes!" said Mrs. Carmichael; "dear me, yes!" And her motherly blue eyes grew quite moist, and she suddenly took Sara in her arms and kissed her. That very night, before she went to sleep, Sara had made the acquaintance of the entire Large Family, and such excitement as she and the monkey had caused in that joyous circle could hardly be described. There was not a child in the nursery, from the Eton boy who was the oldest to the baby who was the youngest, who had not laid some offering on her

shrine. All the older ones knew something of her wonderful story. She had been born in India; she had been
poor and lonely and unhappy, and had lived in a garret and been treated unkindly; and now she was to be
rich and happy, and be taken care of. They were so
sorry for her, and so delighted and curious about her,
all at once. The girls wished to be with her constantly,
and the little boys wished to be told about India; the
second baby, with the short round legs, simply sat
and stared at her and the monkey, possibly wondering
why she had not brought a hand organ with her.

"I shall certainly wake up presently," Sara kept
saying to herself. "This one must be a dream. The
other one turned out to be real, but this couldn't be.
But oh, how happy it is!"

And even when she went to bed in the bright, pretty
room not far from Mrs. Carmichael's own, and Mrs.
Carmichael came and kissed her and patted her and
tucked her in cozily, she was not sure that she would
not wake up in the garret in the morning.

"And oh, Charles, dear," Mrs. Carmichael said to
her husband, when she went downstairs to him, "we
must get that lonely look out of her eyes! It isn't a
child's look at all. I couldn't bear to see it in one of my
own children. What the poor little love must have
had to bear in that dreadful woman's house! But surely
she will forget it in time."

But though the lonely look passed away from Sara's face, she never quite forgot the garret at Miss Minchin's; and indeed she always liked to remember the wonderful night when the tired princess crept upstairs, cold and wet, and, opening the door, found fairyland waiting for her. And there was no one of the many stories she was always being called upon to tell in the nursery of the Large Family which was more popular than that particular one, and there was no one of whom the Large Family were so fond as of Sara. Mr. Carrisford did not die, but recovered, and Sara went to live with him; and no real princess could have been better taken care of than she was. It seemed that the Indian Gentleman could not do enough to make her happy and to repay her for the past, and the Lascar was her devoted slave. As her odd little face grew brighter, it grew so pretty and interesting that Mr. Carrisford used to sit and watch it many an evening, as they sat by the fire together.

They became great friends, and they used to spend hours reading and talking together; and in a very short time there was no pleasanter sight to the Indian Gentleman than Sara sitting in her big chair on the opposite side of the hearth, with a book on her knee and her soft, dark hair tumbling over her warm cheeks. She had a pretty habit of looking up at him suddenly, with a bright smile, and then he would often say to

her, "Are you happy, Sara?" And she would answer, "I feel like a real princess, Uncle Tom." He had told her to call him Uncle Tom.

"There doesn't seem to be anything left to suppose, " she added.

There was a little joke between them that he was a magician, and so could do anything he liked; and it was one of his pleasures to invent plans to surprise her with enjoyments she had not thought of. Scarcely a day passed in which he did not do something new for her. Sometimes she found new flowers in her room,

sometimes a fanciful little gift tucked into some odd corner, sometimes a new book on her pillow. Once as they sat together in the evening they heard the scratch of a heavy paw on the door of the room, and when Sara went to find out what it was, there stood a great dog — a splendid Russian boarhound with a grand silver and gold collar. Stooping to read the inscription upon the collar, Sara was delighted to read the words: "I am Boris; I serve the Princess Sara."

Then there was a sort of fairy nursery arranged for the entertainment of the juvenile members of the

Large Family, who were always coming to see Sara and the Lascar and the monkey. Sara was as fond of the Large Family as they were of her. She soon felt as if she were a member of it, and the companion-ship of the healthy, happy children was very good for her. All the children rather looked up to her and regarded her as the cleverest and most brilliant of creatures, particularly after it was discovered that she not only knew stories of every kind, and could invent new ones at a moment's notice, but that she could help with lessons, speak French and German, and discourse with the Lascar in Hindustani.

It was rather a painful experience for Miss Minchin to watch her ex-pupil's fortunes, as she had the daily opportunity to do, and to feel that she had made a serious mistake from a business point of view. She had even tried to retrieve it by suggesting that Sara's education should be continued under her care, and had gone to the length of making an appeal to the child herself.

"I have always been very fond of you," she said.

Then Sara fixed her eyes upon her and gave her one of her odd looks.

"Have you?" she answered.

"Yes," said Miss Minchin. "Amelia and I have always said you were the cleverest child we had with us, and I am sure we could make you happy — as a parlor boarder."

Sara thought of the garret and the day her ears were boxed, and of that other day — that dreadful, desolate day when she had been told that she belonged to nobody, that she had no home and no friends — and she kept her eyes fixed on Miss Minchin's face.

"You know why I would not stay with you," she said.

And it seems probable that Miss Minchin did, for after that simple answer she had not the boldness to pursue the subject. She merely sent in a bill for the expense of Sara's education and support, and she made it quite large. And because Mr. Carrisford thought Sara would wish it to be paid, it was paid. When Mr. Carmichael paid it, he had a brief interview with Miss Minchin, in which he expressed his opinion with much clearness and force; and it is quite certain that Miss Minchin did not enjoy the conversation.

Sara had been about a month with Mr. Carrisford, and had begun to realize that her happiness was not a dream, when one night the Indian Gentleman saw that she sat a long time with her cheek on her hand looking at the fire.

"What are you supposing, Sara?" he asked. Sara looked up with a bright color on her cheeks.

"I *was* supposing," she said; "I was remembering that hungry day, and a child I saw."

"But there were a great many hungry days," said the Indian Gentleman, with a rather sad tone of voice. "Which hungry day was it?"

"I forgot you didn't know," said Sara. "It was the day I found the things in my garret."

And then she told him the story of the bun shop and the fourpence, and the child who was hungrier than herself; and somehow, though she told it very simply indeed, the Indian Gentleman found it necessary to shade his eyes with his hand and look down at the floor.

"And I was supposing a kind of plan," said Sara, when she had finished. "I was thinking I would like to do something."

"What is it?" said her guardian in a low voice. "You may do anything you like, Princess."

"I was wondering," said Sara "— you know you say I have a great deal of money — and I was wondering if I could go and see the bun woman and tell her that if when hungry children come and sit on the steps or look in the window, particularly on those dreadful days, she would just call them in and give them something to eat, and then send the bills to me and

I would pay them. Could I do that?"

"You shall do it tomorrow morning," said the Indian Gentleman.

"Thank you," said Sara. "You see I know what it is to be hungry, and it is very hard when one can't even *pretend* it away."

"Yes, yes, my dear," said the Indian Gentleman. "Yes, it must be. Try to forget it. Come and sit on this footstool near my knee, and only remember you are a princess."

"Yes," said Sara, "and I can give buns and bread to the Populace." And she went and sat on the stool, and the Indian Gentleman (he used to like her to call him that sometimes — in fact, very often) drew her small, dark head down upon his knee and stroked her hair.

The next morning a carriage drew up before the door of the bakery shop, and a gentleman and a little girl got out — oddly enough, just as the bun woman was putting a tray of smoking-hot buns into the window. When Sara entered the shop, the woman turned and looked at her and, leaving the buns, came and stood behind the counter. For a moment she looked at Sara very hard indeed, and then her good-natured face lighted up.

"I'm that sure I remember you, miss," she said. "And yet —"

"Yes," said Sara, "once you gave me six buns for fourpence, and —"

"And you gave five of 'em to a beggar child," said the woman. "I've always remembered it. I couldn't make it out at first. I beg pardon, sir, but there's not many young people that notices a hungry face in that way, and I've thought of it many a time. Excuse the liberty, miss, but you look rosier and better than you did that day."

"I am better, thank you," said Sara, "and — and I am happier, and I have come to ask you to do something for me."

"Me, miss!" exclaimed the woman. "Why, bless you yes, miss! What can I do?"

And then Sara made her little proposal, and the woman listened to it with an astonished face.

"Why, bless me!" she said, when she had heard it all. "Yes, miss, it'll be a pleasure to me to do it. I am a working woman myself, and can't afford to do much on my own account, and there's sights of trouble on every side; but if you'll excuse me, I'm bound to say I've given many a bit of bread away since that wet afternoon, just thinkin' of you. An' how wet an' cold you was, an' how you looked — an' yet you give away your hot buns as if you was a princess."

The Indian Gentleman smiled involuntarily, and Sara smiled a little too. "She looked so hungry," she said. "She was hungrier than I was."

"She was starving," said the woman. "Many's the time she's told me of it since — how she sat there in the wet and felt as if a wolf was atearing at her poor young insides."

"Oh, have you seen her since then?" exclaimed Sara. "Do you know where she is?"

"Do I know!" said the woman. "Why, she's in that there back room now, miss, an' has been for a month. An' a decent, well-meaning girl she's going to turn out, an' such a help to me in the day shop an' in the kitchen as you'd scarce believe, knowing how she's lived."

She stepped to the door of the little back parlor and spoke, and the next minute a girl came out and followed her behind the counter. It was actually the beggar child, clean and neatly clothed, and looking as if she had not been hungry for a long time. She looked shy, but she had a nice face now that she was no longer a savage and the wild look had gone from her eyes. And she knew Sara in an instant, and stood and looked at her as if she could never look enough.

"You see," said the woman, "I told her to come

here when she was hungry, and when she'd come I'd give her odd jobs to do. An' I found she was willing, an' somehow I got to like her; an' the end of it was I've given her a place an' a home, an' she helps me, an' behaves as well an' is as thankful as a girl can be. Her name's Anne; she has no other."

The two children stood and looked at each other a few moments. In Sara's eyes a new thought was growing.

"I'm glad you have such a good home," she said. "Perhaps Mrs. Brown will let you give the buns and bread to the hungry children — perhaps you would like to do it because you know what it is to be hungry, too."

"Yes, miss," said the girl.

And somehow Sara felt as if the girl understood her, though she said nothing more, and only stood still and looked and looked after her as she went out of the shop and got into the carriage and drove away.